Priya
the Polar Bear Fairy

by Daisy Meadows

ORCHARD

www.rainbowmagicbooks.co.uk

Fairyland Palace

Sparkle Forest

Snow Leopard Enclosure

The Girls' Cabin

Elephant Bath

TAIL AND TRUNK SAFARI PARK

Jack Frost's Spell

I want a zoo – don't say I'm wrong!
But finding pets takes far too long.
Fill each cage with stinky straw.
I will get what I'm wishing for!

In Sparkle Forest every day,
Peculiar creatures run and play.
The animals are rare – so what?
Get in there and steal the lot!

Contents

Chapter One
Three Bears

Kirsty Tate was dreaming.

In the dream, her best friend Rachel Walker was calling her name, but every time Kirsty tried to reply, an elephant trumpeted loudly.

"Kirsty!" called Rachel again.

This time, the elephant's trumpeting was so loud that it woke Kirsty up. She smiled and sat up in bed. Rachel was sitting up in the bed on the other side of the room. There really was an elephant trumpeting in the distance, and now Kirsty remembered why. She and Rachel were staying at the Tail and Trunk Safari Park, just outside Wetherbury Village. They had won a picture competition,

and the prize was a stay at the safari park.

"Ahmed said he'd pick us up first thing this morning," said Kirsty, swinging her legs out of bed. "I wonder which animals we'll be visiting first today."

Ahmed was their tour guide. He had already shown them lots of wonderful animals at the safari park, and he had promised that there were plenty more to see.

"And I wonder which of our fairy friends we'll be seeing today," Rachel added, peeping out of the window. "The Endangered Animals Fairies really need our help, Kirsty."

The girls got dressed, chatting about the magical adventure they had shared the day before. Etta the Elephant Fairy had taken them to Sparkle Forest in Fairyland, where they had met the Endangered Animals Fairies. The fairies looked after animal habitats in the human world, and kept endangered species safe in Fairyland. But while Rachel and Kirsty were in Sparkle Forest, Jack Frost had appeared with his goblins and kidnapped the fairies' magical companions. To make things even more complicated, the goblins had disobeyed their master and taken the enchanted animals off to the human world.

"We can't let Jack Frost put the animals in cages for his own private zoo," said Kirsty in a determined voice.

"We just have to find those goblins before Jack Frost does," Rachel added.

"Or animal habitats will be spoiled and rare animals will be in more danger than ever."

They were interrupted by Mrs Walker popping her head around the door.

"Morning!" she said. "Oh good, you're up. Ahmed will be here soon."

"We can't wait," said Kirsty.

"I spoke to your parents last night," Mrs Walker added, smiling at Kirsty. "They're happy for you to stay with us at the safari park for two more days."

Rachel and Kirsty shared a happy hug. Just then, they heard a jeep pull up outside.

"Ahmed's here," called Mr Walker.

The girls ran outside, picking up some toast on the way. Ahmed was sitting in his tiger-striped jeep, and the engine was purring.

"Good morning," he said, flashing them a broad smile. "I hear that you're going to be around for a few more days. Fantastic!"

"Where are we going first?" asked Rachel excitedly.

"I thought I'd take you to visit the polar bears this morning," said Ahmed.

"Oh yes, I'd love that," said Kirsty as she and Rachel put on their seatbelts.

The jeep rumbled towards the heart of the safari park. Even though it was early, the sun was already extremely hot. Many animals were still sheltering inside their

enclosures.

"I think polar bears are beautiful," said Rachel, in between bites of toast. "I love their white fur."

"Actually, polar bears have transparent fur," said Ahmed. "And did you know that their skin is black?"

"No, we didn't," said Rachel and Kirsty, sharing a smile.

They had already learned that Ahmed was full of amazing facts about all their favourite animals.

"The polar bear keeper, Elkie, will be

able to tell you lots more," he said. "She's been here ever since the bears arrived, and there's nothing she doesn't know about them."

A few minutes later, Ahmed stopped the jeep on one of the park's wide paths.

"We have to go the rest of the way on foot," he said.

He led Rachel and Kirsty along a narrow walkway that went all around

the polar bear enclosure. Two adult polar bears and a wriggly little cub were lying on a rock beside a pool. A low archway was cut into the rock behind them. The three polar bears were panting in the morning sunshine.

"The adults are called Charlie and Matilda, after two of Elkie's favourite books," said Ahmed. "And the baby is called James."

Rachel and Kirsty smiled. They loved those books too.

"Don't they miss having ice and snow?" Kirsty asked. "They look a bit hot."

"Polar bears are very adaptable," said Ahmed. "But actually, we've made sure they have ice too. That archway in the rock leads to a special ice-cave habitat.

Priya

I'm not sure why they're not in there on this hot morning, actually. Come on, I'll show you."

Chapter Two
Melting Magic

Ahmed led the girls around the walkway and down some steps.

"We have a viewing gallery so visitors can see the polar bears enjoying their natural habitat," he explained. "It's a shame it has to be inside, but that's the only way for us to keep it cold enough."

They reached the bottom of the

steps and found themselves in a large
underground chamber. One long wall
was made of glass, through which they
could see a rugged cave built from ice
blocks. The archway they had seen
outside was high up, and ledges of ice led
down to a pool.

Ahmed stopped so suddenly that the girls bumped into him.

"Something's wrong,"  he said in a worried voice. "The ledges should be covered in a layer of snow. And there are usually lumps of ice floating in the pool. Where has the snow gone? And why is the water level so high?"

Now that the girls looked more closely, they could see that water was running down the inside of the glass and dripping from the ice blocks.

"It's melting," said Rachel in a horrified voice.

"No wonder the polar bears didn't

want to come in here," said Rachel. "They must be really confused."

"I don't blame them," said Ahmed. "I'm confused too."

The girls exchanged a sad glance. They knew that this was happening because Jack Frost had stolen the fairies' animal companions. Until they could help find the missing animals, habitats would continue to be in danger.

"I must go to HQ and find Elkie," said Ahmed. "She'll want to know if there's something wrong with the enclosure. Do you two mind waiting?"

"Of course not," said Kirsty. "We'll be fine. The most important thing is to look after the polar bears."

Ahmed dashed away, and the best friends peered through the glass.

"The ice is melting fast," said Rachel. "Soon it will just be a room full of warm water."

"This is like when the elephant habitat was damaged yesterday," said Kirsty. "It makes me so cross that the

polar bears' home is in danger, all because of that mean Jack Frost."

"Hey, look at that little ice block on the edge," said Rachel suddenly. "It's glowing."

The girls would have known that magical glow anywhere. Thrilled and excited, they watched the small, white block glow brighter and brighter. Then it burst into tiny pieces of ice, each one shaped like a miniature polar bear, with Priya the Polar Bear Fairy fluttering among them. Her dark hair, maroon leggings and deep green jacket looked striking against the dazzling ice. She smiled at the girls, beckoning them to join her.

"We can't come in," said Rachel, spreading her arms wide. "There isn't a door."

Priya laughed, and the girls could see her breath misting in the air. She waved her wand, and the glass of the viewing window started to shimmer like liquid silver. At the same moment, the girls felt the warm tingle of magic upon them. They shrank to fairy size and rose into the air on cobweb-thin wings.

Hand in hand, the girls flew towards

27

the shimmering glass. It was like passing
through a silvery waterfall. A second later,
they were inside the polar bears' ice cave.

"Who needs doors when you have
magic?" said Priya, smiling. "I'm glad
to see you. Etta told me that she found
Stampy here at the safari park, so I've
come to look for Snowy. Have you got

the time to help me?"

"Of course," said Rachel and Kirsty together.

Quickly, they explained what had happened. Priya looked around at the melting ice with a frown.

"This is happening all over the human world," she said. "We must find Snowy. Things will only return to normal when she is back home in Sparkle Forest."

Chapter Three
Bearnapped!

At that moment the polar bear cub, James, came tumbling down the icy ledges from the archway above. He plopped into the water with a splash, and the fairies giggled as he scrambled out on to the ice.

"He's full of fun," said Priya, fluttering down beside the baby and ruffling his fur. "Just like Snowy."

Just then, a second cub came rolling down the ice ledges and splashed into the water.

"I thought there was only one cub," said Rachel.

Spluttering and panting, the polar bear cub reached the ice and began to scramble out.

"Snowy!" Priya exclaimed in a delighted voice.

Rachel and Kirsty gasped. Now that the cub was out of the water, they could see a magical glow clinging to the tips of her fur. Just like Stampy, now that she was in the human world she had grown to the size of an ordinary animal.

Priya darted forwards to greet Snowy, but suddenly a goblin sprang out from under an icy ledge. He jumped in front of Priya and shoved her backwards. She landed hard on an ice block.

"Priya!" cried Rachel, rushing to help her.

"I'm OK," said Priya, standing up and rubbing her leg.

"That was really mean," said Kirsty, fluttering in front of the goblin.

"I don't care," said the goblin, blowing a raspberry at her. "Buzz off so I can

play with my polar bear."

"Snowy isn't your polar bear," said
Priya. "Animals don't belong to us. We
share our world with them."

"Blah blah blah," said the goblin
rudely. "She's mine and I'm keeping her."

"We won't let you," said Rachel, flying
to Kirsty's side.

The goblin snorted with laughter. Then he turned around and squealed.

"Two polar bears?" he exclaimed. "It's my lucky day!"

He lunged towards them, and the animals cringed in fear. The goblin tucked one cub under each arm and turned back to the fairies.

"They're both mine now, and you can't stop me from taking them."

"Can't you see that they're scared?" asked Priya. "Don't you care?"

For the first time, the goblin looked unsure of himself.

He frowned in confusion.

"But they're so sweet," he said. "I won't hurt them."

At that moment, a terrible roar echoed around the ice cave. They all looked up. The polar bear mummy, Matilda, was standing in the archway with her big, sharp teeth bared.

"She wants her cub back," said Priya.

The goblin's knobbly knees started knocking together.

"These cubs are mine," he squeaked in a trembling voice.

Matilda roared again, and started lumbering down the ledges towards the goblin.

"He should put those cubs down right now," said Priya.

Suddenly, the goblin stopped shaking. His face took on a smug expression.

"I just remembered that Jack Frost gave me a little bit of magic," he said. "Polar bears are no match for me."

There was a blue flash, and the goblin disappeared – with the cubs!

"Where did he go?" Priya cried.

Kirsty thought quickly.

"I bet he hasn't gone far," she said.
"The magic Jack Frost gave the goblins
was only enough to make their journey
to the Ice Castle faster. This goblin has
already used some of it to come to the
human world. He doesn't have much left."

Priya hugged her tightly.

"You're right," she said. "Let's go and check the outside habitat."

The three fairies swooped upwards past Matilda and through the archway. They saw the goblin at once. He was standing on top of the highest rock, sticking his tongue out at Charlie, the daddy polar bear. Charlie roared in a rage.

"Give Snowy back!" cried Kirsty, zooming towards the goblin.

"I just want to take care of them," the goblin yelled. "They can live with me in Goblin Grotto."

"But that won't work," Priya exclaimed. "Polar bears need lots of space to run and play. They need fish to eat and places to clamber and swim. There's nowhere like that in Goblin Grotto."

The goblin stuck out his bottom lip stubbornly.

"I've got a blow-up paddling pool and a climbing frame and a box of fish

41

fingers," he said. "What more could a polar bear want?"

"All this," said Rachel, sweeping her arm around the wonderful habitat.

The goblin looked around, and then his shoulders slumped a little.

For a moment, Rachel and Kirsty thought that he was going to let go of the cubs. But then Charlie roared again. There was another flash of blue light, and the goblin disappeared.

Chapter Four
Jack Frost Appears

"Over there!" Rachel shouted, spotting the goblin on a rock in the middle of the pool.

Charlie dived into the water and swam towards the rock. With a yelp of alarm, the goblin disappeared again. This time he reappeared on a ledge halfway up the side of the habitat.

"That blue flash seemed weaker than the others," said Kirsty. "Did you notice? I think the magic Jack Frost gave him is almost gone."

"That would explain why he hasn't magicked himself out of this habitat," said Rachel. "He hasn't got enough magic left."

Matilda had come back from the ice cave now, and she and Charlie let out furious roars that made the air shake. The goblin was still high on the ledge with the cubs struggling under his arms. He looked petrified.

"I don't think he has any magic left to get himself down from there," said Kirsty. "And look – Charlie and Matilda are starting to climb up towards him."

James's parents were scrambling from

44

rock to rock, getting closer to the goblin with every moment. Rachel had an idea. She zoomed across the habitat and hovered in front of the goblin. Kirsty and Priya were close behind her.

"Will you promise to hand Snowy and James back if Priya magics you out of here?" Rachel asked.

Priya

The goblin nodded vehemently, and Priya waved her wand. Instantly, the goblin was standing on the walkway above the habitat. The fairies flew up to join him as Charlie and Matilda roared again.

"Oh, my knobbly knees!" said the goblin, gasping for breath. "Oh, my googly eyes! Oh, my wobbly nostrils! I don't like grown-up polar bears."

"You can't blame them for being cross," said Priya in a stern voice. "You took their baby."

"I'm sorry," the goblin wailed. "I'll never do it again."

"So will you give Snowy and James back?" Rachel asked.

"But they're so sweet," said the goblin. "Can't I keep one?"

"You promised," Rachel reminded him.

But at that moment, a crack of thunder ripped the air and Jack Frost appeared between the goblin and the fairies. His eyes were crackling with fury.

"Weakling!" he yelled at the goblin. "Traitor! Making promises to fairies? Taking my polar bear? I'll have you scrubbing mouldy bins for a year!"

"Leave him alone," said Kirsty. "He was about to do the right thing."

Jack Frost whipped around and snarled at her. "There's only one right thing for a goblin," he said. "And that's to do whatever I say. Now, which one of these furballs is the magic one?"

No one replied. Jack Frost's eyes narrowed. "Fine," he went on. "I can work it out for myself – when they're safely in a cage. You will never see either of these cubs again."

"But James belongs here with his parents," Kirsty exclaimed. "You can't take him."

"I can do whatever I want," said Jack Frost, curling his lip.

He turned back to the goblin and raised his wand.

"Quick, hold on to me," Rachel whispered to Kirsty and Priya. "He's about to disappear, and we're going with him!"

Rachel grabbed the hem of Jack Frost's cloak as another loud crack of thunder echoed around them. The fairies saw a bright-blue flash. Then they slammed into something cold and hard.

Feeling dizzy, Rachel sat up. She was sitting on a stone floor in a long corridor. She instantly recognised the dark walls dripping with water, and the smell of mildew in the air. They were inside Jack Frost's ice castle.

"Ouch," said a familiar voice.

Kirsty sat up on one side of her, looking dazed. Priya was on her other side, rubbing her head and groaning.

"That is nowhere near as nice as fairy magic," said Kirsty.

"Shh!" said Priya. "Look!"

Jack Frost was standing a few feet away, with his back to them.

"Now, goblin," he said. "Hand over those cubs so I can put them in a nice cage for the rest of their lives."

Chapter Five
Rebel Goblin

"Thank goodness he didn't notice that we hitched a ride," said Kirsty.

They crawled a little closer and peeped around the flowing blue cloak. The goblin was cowering back against a damp wall with his arms around the cubs.

"But – but – won't they be unhappy in a cage?" he said in a squeaky voice.

"They need space ... and water ... and fish."

The fairies exchanged looks of surprise. It sounded as if the goblin had really learned something while he'd been at Tail and Trunk.

"What are you gibbering about, you nincompoop?" Jack Frost bellowed.

"They'll share a cage with a bit of straw and be grateful for it!"

The goblin stared at his master, his knees knocking together again. He was clearly terrified, but he wasn't giving up the animals.

"I've got an idea," Rachel whispered. "We just have to hope that the goblin really does care about the polar bears."

Taking a deep breath, she peered out from behind Jack Frost and made sure that the goblin could see her. His eyes widened. Rachel gathered the hem of Jack Frost's cloak in one hand and pointed to it. Then she held up three fingers and counted down. Three … two … one …

"RUN!" she shouted.

Everything happened at once. The

goblin darted away, Jack Frost raised his
wand and Rachel tugged at his cloak.

"AARGH!" Jack Frost yelled as he was
pulled backwards.

A flash of blue lightning from his wand
hit the roof of the corridor, bounced back
and hit his wand. It was instantly burned
to a crisp.

"My wand!" he shrieked, struggling to get up. "You midget menaces! You pint-sized pests!"

The fairies clung on to his cloak, trying to keep him on the ground.

"We won't let you lock animals in cages," Kirsty cried.

"You'll never have that zoo!" Priya added.

"GRRRR!" Jack Frost cried. "You'll be sorry for this, you interfering little busybodies!"

He yanked himself free of them, jumped to his feet and sprinted after the goblin. The fairies followed close behind.

Rachel and Kirsty had never been on such an incredible chase. They raced through every inch of the castle, through long corridors, up and down winding staircases, under tables and beds, along secret passages, over the castle turrets, around the towers and across the icy courtyard. Goblin guards lined the way, cheering and booing, and throwing anything they could find at the fairies, from stale buns to snotty tissues.

The chase had been going for half
an hour when the goblin raced into the
castle kitchen, sending trays of pondweed
muffins and frogspawn jelly flying into
the air. Jack Frost skidded into the
kitchen, with the fairies close behind.
The goblin backed away, panting, and
stopped in front of the window. The cubs
whimpered.

"You're trapped,"
wheezed Jack Frost.

He took a step
towards the goblin.
Snowy and James
hid their faces in the
goblin's arms.

"Oh no, you don't,"
said Priya.

She pointed her

wand at the goblin, and he rose into the
air with the cubs still in his arms. The
kitchen window opened, and the goblin
floated out and disappeared from sight.

"Get me a new wand!" Jack Frost
shrieked, hopping with rage.

The fairies swooped out of the open
window and saw the goblin running
across the frost-covered lawn.

"He's heading for the woods," said
Kirsty. "Follow him!"

Jack Frost's enraged yells faded behind
them. They flew as fast as their wings
could flutter, but they were all tired from
the long chase, and the goblin had a
head start. Before they could catch up
with him, he reached the woods and
disappeared into the thick, snowy trees.

Panting, Priya sank to the cold ground.

"I can't fly any further," she said. "It's no good – we've lost Snowy."

"We haven't," said Rachel in a firm voice. "We just need to rest and catch our breath."

Together, she and Kirsty helped Priya into the woods. They sat down on a tree root and Priya magicked up some water for them all.

"These woods are enormous," said Priya. "We'll never find the goblin here!"

Chapter Five
Breakfast with the Bears

"Rachel and I have been to these woods lots of times," said Kirsty, thinking back to some of the magical adventures they had shared with the fairies. "We know a few of the hiding places in here. I'm sure the goblin can't have got far."

"And while we're here in Fairyland, time will stand still in the human world," added Rachel. "So Charlie and Matilda won't be worrying about James."

Priya relaxed a little. "That's true," she said. "That does make me feel better. Thank you, Rachel and Kirsty. You're wonderful friends."

"Come on," said Kirsty, standing up. "Let's start looking."

"You don't need to look," said a miserable, squawky voice. "I'm here."

The goblin stepped out from behind a tree, still carrying the cubs. He put them down on the ground, and Snowy rushed towards Priya.

"Oh, Snowy!" she cried as he jumped into her arms. "I've missed you so much!"

He nuzzled his wet nose into her neck,

and she laughed. Rachel and Kirsty
smiled, and then turned to look at James.
He pressed himself against the goblin's
legs as if he was saying goodbye. Then
he ambled over to join Snowy and the
fairies.

"I think you've made a friend after all,"
said Rachel.

"I'm going to be in so much trouble

with Jack Frost," the goblin wailed.

"Oh no, you won't," said Priya in a firm voice. "I'm going to magic you home to Goblin Grotto. Jack Frost will be too busy finding a new wand and searching for the other two magical animals to worry about looking for

you. But first, I have something for you."

She waved her wand, and a fine silver chain appeared around the goblin's neck. A silver pendant in the shape of a polar bear cub dangled from the chain. A smile spread over the goblin's face, and then he disappeared in a flurry of fairy dust.

"He's safely home," said Priya. "It's time that everyone else was home too. Goodbye, my lovely friends, and thank you!"

Silvery sparkles whirled around them, and the snowy forest disappeared. When the glitter cleared, Rachel and Kirsty were back in the viewing chamber of

the Tail and Trunk polar bear ice cave.
The glass was solid again, and they had
returned to human size.

"Look," said Kirsty, pressing her hand
against the glass.

James was sitting on some soft snow on
the other side of the glass. He placed his
paw on the glass, by Kirsty's hand.

"I think that's his way of saying thank

you," said Rachel with a smile.

The ice cave looked very different. Lumps of ice were floating in the water, and snow was heaped on the ice blocks. The water level had gone down too.

"No more melting ice here, thank goodness," said Kirsty.

Just then, Matilda and Charlie appeared in the archway at the top of the cave. They roared, but these were happy roars. James plunged into the water, and his parents tumbled down the ice and splashed in beside him. The three bears rolled in the water playfully, happy to be together again.

Footsteps made Rachel and Kirsty turn around. Ahmed came hurrying down the stairs with a redheaded young woman.

"You see," he said to her. "It's all

completely—" He gaped at the snow and
the happy polar bears. "Er, completely
fine," he finished.

The young woman raised her eyebrows
at him.

"Is this a joke?" she asked.

Rachel and Kirsty felt uneasy. They

didn't want Ahmed to get into trouble.

"It's not a joke," said Rachel.

Ahmed seemed to notice them for the first time.

"This is Elkie, the polar bear keeper," he said unhappily to the girls. "Elkie, meet Rachel and Kirsty."

"Hi, girls," said Elkie.

"The ice cave really was melting," said Kirsty. "We all saw it."

"Maybe the temperature control failed for a while and then somehow fixed itself," said Rachel.

Elkie nodded. "Probably just a computer glitch," she said. "The main thing is that the bears are OK. Now, as I'm here, how about helping me to feed them and learning a few facts?"

"Yes please!" said the girls together.

Ahmed grinned, and he and Elkie led the way up the stairs. Rachel and Kirsty held back a little.

"What an adventure!" said Rachel in a low voice. "I really thought Jack Frost was going to catch the goblin when he trapped him in the kitchen. And I could hardly believe it when the goblin decided to help us."

"I'm just happy that we got Snowy

back safely," said Kirsty. "But there are still two magical animals missing, and Jack Frost's goblins could have taken them anywhere. I hope we find them soon."

"We have to stay alert and keep looking out for trouble," said Rachel. "I've got a feeling that our next adventure is just around the corner!"

The End

Now it's time for Kirsty and Rachel to help ...

Chelsea the Chimpanzee Fairy

Read on for a sneak peek ...

"Do you think they've noticed us?" Rachel Walker asked as she and her best friend, Kirsty, watched a chimpanzee high up in a tree.

"I hope not," said Kirsty Tate, whispering. "I want to see them play."

They were on their third day at Tail and Trunk Safari Park and the park manager, Ahmed, had brought them here to see the mischief that the chimpanzees got up to at Cheeky Chimp Corner – the ape enclosure. There was a long wooden bench beneath some trees. Earlier that morning, Rachel and Kirsty had helped Ahmed put out grapes, bananas and nuts for the animals. Then they'd gone back to Ahmed's truck, which was painted in orange and black tiger stripes.

Now, the girls sat in the back with a fluffy zebra-print blanket over their knees. Ahmed had passed them each a fruit smoothie that he'd made earlier.

"Grapes and kiwi fruit, mixed with yogurt and almond milk," he said. "Drink up!"

The girls each took a sip through pink and yellow striped paper straws.

"Yum!" Kirsty said.

"Delicious," Rachel said, taking another sip.

The two of them were the very best friends in the whole village of

Wetherbury. They'd come to this safari park on the edge of town with Rachel's parents, Mr and Mrs Walker. They were staying in a little wooden hut with gingham curtains and they had offered to help Ahmed around the park. The two girls would get up extra early each morning, to help the park manager change the animals' straw and put out fresh food for them. It was a magical start to the day, before the park gates opened to visitors. Magic seemed to follow the two best friends around wherever they went.

Ahmed was watching the chimpanzees carefully, his hat tipped back on his head. "Did you know …" he began to say. Rachel and Kirsty shared a secret glance and smiled. "… chimpanzees share ninety-eight per cent of their DNA with humans." Ahmed loved his facts, even more than he loved the animals of Tail and Trunk Safari Park.

Suddenly, the back of the truck gave a lurch. Rachel nearly dropped her smoothie! There was a scrabbling sound as something ran away.

"What was that?" Ahmed cried, leaping out from behind the wheel. Kirsty and Rachel carefully placed their smoothies in the truck's cup holders and scrambled out after him. A tiny, hairy shape dragged its feet across the grass and heaved itself over the fence towards the Cheeky Chimp Corner. His furry little hands glowed in the morning sunshine, but it wasn't sunlight glinting off his fur. The glow looked almost magical.

"Oh no!" Rachel whispered, pulling Kirsty behind a tree. "I think it's Bouncy

Bobo. That glow – it looks like Jack Frost's magic."

Bouncy Bobo was a chimpanzee from Sparkle Forest in Fairyland. Rachel and Kirsty had gone there with Etta the Elephant Fairy, and they had met the rest of the Endangered Animals Fairies. At Sparkle Forest, all sorts of animals from around the world lived together in the forest glade, even ones that were endangered in Kirsty and Rachel's world. Then Jack Frost had arrived! With the help of his naughty goblins, he'd captured the four fairies' special magical animals – an elephant, a snow leopard, a polar bear … and Bobo, the bouncy chimpanzee. Rachel and Kirsty had helped get two of the animals back to Sparkle Forest, but there were still two more to save, and one of them was Bobo.

"What is that naughty chimpanzee doing?" Ahmed suddenly cried, pulling out his phone to take photos. "We don't like to see the animals stealing. Wait till I tell the park owner about this!"

Bobo had dragged himself up onto the chimpanzees' picnic table and stole a banana out of another chimpanzee's fist.

Read **Chelsea the Chimpanzee Fairy** to find out what adventures are in store for Kirsty and Rachel!

Calling all parents, carers and teachers!
The Rainbow Magic fairies are here to help
your child enter the magical world of reading.
Whatever reading stage they are at, there's
a Rainbow Magic book for everyone!
Here is Lydia the Reading Fairy's guide to
supporting your child's journey at all levels.

Starting Out

Our Rainbow Magic Beginner Readers are perfect for first-time readers who are just beginning to develop reading skills and confidence. Approved by teachers, they contain a full range of educational levelling, as well as lively full-colour illustrations.

1

Developing Readers

Rainbow Magic Early Readers contain longer stories and wider vocabulary for building stamina and growing confidence. These are adaptations of our most popular Rainbow Magic stories, specially developed for younger readers in conjunction with an Early Years reading consultant, with full-colour illustrations.

2

Going Solo

The Rainbow Magic chapter books - a mixture of series and one-off specials - contain accessible writing to encourage your child to venture into reading independently. These highly collectible and much-loved magical stories inspire a love of reading to last a lifetime.

3

www.rainbowmagicbooks.co.uk

"Rainbow Magic got my daughter reading chapter books. Great sparkly covers, cute fairies and traditional stories full of magic that she found impossible to put down" - Mother of Edie (6 years)

"Florence LOVES the Rainbow Magic books. She really enjoys reading now" - Mother of Florence (6 years)

The Rainbow Magic
Reading Challenge

Well done, fairy friend – you have completed the book!
This book was worth 5 points.

See how far you have climbed on the
Reading Rainbow opposite.

The more books you read, the more points you will get,
and the closer you will be to becoming a Fairy Princess!

How to get your Reading Rainbow
1. Cut out the coin below
2. Go to the Rainbow Magic website
3. Download and print out your poster
4. Add your coin and climb up the Reading Rainbow!

There's all this and lots more at
www.rainbowmagicbooks.co.uk

You'll find activities, competitions, stories, a special
newsletter and complete profiles of all the
Rainbow Magic fairies. Find a fairy with your name!